THE CANTERBURY TALES

THE CANTERBURY TALES

By Geoffrey Chaucer

Adapted by Diana Stewart
Illustrated by Dan Hubrich

RSVP
RAINTREE STECK-VAUGHN
PUBLISHERS
The Steck-Vaughn Company

Austin, Texas

Library of Congress Number: 80-22141

Library of Congress Cataloging-in-Publication Data

Stewart, Diana.
  The Canterbury tales.

  (Raintree short classics series)
  CONTENTS: Introduction.—The prologue.—The
pardoner's tale.—[etc.]
    1. Children's stories, American. [1. Middle
Ages—Fiction. 2. England—Fiction. 3. Short
stories] I. Chaucer, Geoffrey, d. 1400. Canter-
bury tales. Selections. II. Hubrich, Dan.
III. Title. IV. Series: Raintree short classics.
PZ7.G84878Can   [Fic]   80-22141

ISBN 0-8172-1666-9 hardcover library binding

ISBN 0-8114-6821-6 softcover binding

Device on front cover courtesy of F.H. Ehmcke,
Graphic Trade Symbols by German Designers,
Dover Publications

18 19 20   99 98

CONTENTS

INTRODUCTION

Geoffrey Chaucer wrote *The Canterbury Tales* almost six hundred years ago. He wrote them in rhyme in the language of the time — known today as Middle English. There were no dictionaries then, and people spelled words any way they wanted to. Here are the first few lines of the Prologue just the way Chaucer wrote it:

> Whan that Aprille with his shoures soote
> The droghte of March hath perced to the roote,
> And bathed every veyne in swich licour
> Oh which vertu engendred is the flour;

The language of *The Canterbury Tales* may be strange, but the people Chaucer wrote about are not that different from people today. That is why his tales are still so popular. The people he writes about have the same thoughts and desires as the modern reader. They are greedy for money or love, or they just want to be happy and entertained.

When the story begins, thirty pilgrims — strangers to each other — meet one night in an inn in Southwark, a town just outside of London. They are all on their way to the city of Canterbury to visit the church where St. Thomas was killed. It has become a religious shrine where travelers come to worship.

Now Southwark is about sixty miles from Canterbury. In those days, it would have been a four-day ride by horse. What Chaucer planned was to have each of his characters tell four stories — two on the way to the shrine and two on the way back. That would have been over a hundred tales in all.

He worked on these short stories over a period of several years, but when he died, only twenty-one of the tales were completed. There also are bits and pieces of other tales. He had not put all the tales in any set order, nor did he indicate which person told the winning tale. That is now left up to the reader to decide.

THE PROLOGUE

Here Begins the Book of the Tales of Canterbury

April in England is beautiful. The cold and rain of March are gone. The wind is gentle and the sun is warm. The soft showers bring out the new flowers of spring. After a cold, hard winter, people long to leave their homes and travel out in the sunshine. They love to visit far places and worship at distant religious shrines. In England the place where they like to travel best is Canterbury. So it was with me.

On just such an April day, I left my home in London to make the journey to Canterbury. The first night I found an inn in Southwark. The inn was crowded with other travelers — twenty-nine in all. And all of these people were pilgrims, like myself, on their way to Canterbury.

Fortunately the inn was large. We each had good rooms, and there was plenty of space in the stables for our horses. That evening I met the other guests. They were a good, merry group, and I soon made friends with them. Since we were all traveling to Canterbury the next day, we decided to ride together.

My companions were a mixed group. These travelers came from every rank of society — from the common workers to the noble knights. Some were rich and some were poor. But let me tell you a little about them, and you will see what I mean.

There was a brave knight who loved truth and honor and freedom; a handsome young squire; a nun who sat and smiled quietly; a merchant with a forked beard dressed in bright clothes; a wise lawyer — a very good man; a sailor from the west part of England. There was a cook, a doctor, a carpenter — oh, so many more. Two of my new friends caught my special interest.

One of these was a housewife from near the town of Bath. Sadly, she was deaf in one ear. Also, she had gaps in her teeth. But she was still a pretty woman and had had five husbands in all, all of them dead now. She was very skillful in weaving, and I swear, the scarves she wore on her head must have weighed ten pounds. The good lady had traveled a great deal. She had made many pilgrimages — even to Rome and Jerusalem. Oh, how she loved to joke and laugh, and she knew everything there was to know about love — from a lot of experience, I think.

Another of my companions was a pardoner. His blond hair was long and wavy. He tied some of it in bunches on the top of his head. The rest he left hanging down in back over his shoulders. His eyes were small and shining like a rabbit's, and his voice sounded like a bleating goat. He carried a bag stuffed full with pardons he had brought from Rome.

Also in his bag were religious items. He claimed that one piece of cloth came from the sail of St. Peter's boat — the boat he had used to carry Jesus across the sea. He also had pig bones he claimed could cure sickness. As he traveled around, he would sell such items to poor country parsons. He often made more money in a day than those poor churchmen made in two months.

These people, then, were my traveling companions.

That night all thirty of us sat and ate together. The host of the inn gave us his best food and made us very comfortable. He was a big jolly man who laughed often and told us jokes and stories.

After we had eaten and paid our bills, he said to us: "I don't know when I have seen such a happy group of people. You are all very welcome here. Now, I have thought up a game for you to play tomorrow as you travel to Canterbury. It will make you happy and cost you very little. Tell me now if you will agree to the plan I have in mind."

We quickly voted to agree to whatever our host suggested. "Tell us your plan," I said.

"Listen, then, ladies and gentlemen," he replied. "All of you have traveled a great deal. You have all been many places and seen many wonderful things. I know that tomorrow you will tell each other stories of your travels as you ride. What I suggest is this: Each of you tell your tales. And the one who tells the best story shall win this prize. On your way home, you will stop here again. The winner shall have his room and meal paid for by the rest of you. I will go along with you and be the judge. Do you all agree to let me decide the winner?"

We agreed, and the host brought us wine to drink. Afterwards, we all went to bed to get ready for our journey the next day.

In the morning we set out together on our pilgrimage. Once on our way, our host had us draw straws to see which person would tell his story first. The knight won the first draw. After him came the cook, then the lawyer, and then the nun, and so on.

Some of the tales they told were long. Some were short. Each person did his best to make his story full of good teachings. Most of us tried to make the tales as interesting and entertaining as possible. And in this way we made our journey pass quickly and pleasantly.

Three of the stories I will tell you now, because they are

filled with good, moral teachings and are sure to amuse you. Good friends, I know you will forgive me if I repeat these tales just as they were told. Please do not be shocked if the people in the tales are cruel or wicked. God made people human — whether they are rich or poor, whether they are of noble birth or low birth, whether they are churchmen or not. To tell these stories well, I must let the people speak for themselves.

Here first, then, is the tale told to us by the wife of Bath.

THE WIFE OF BATH'S TALE

"Good friends," said the wife, "I want to tell you about the troubles you will find in marriage. I speak from good experience. Since I was twelve years old, I have had five husbands. And if I can find him, I will have a sixth.

"Isn't it wonderful that God tells us it is good to marry? And he doesn't set a limit on the number of husbands we can have — as long as we only marry them one at a time, that is.

"But let me tell you the truth. Three of my husbands were good and two were bad. The good ones were old and rich, and I knew how to handle them. I nagged them horribly. Then they were happy to buy me anything I wanted just to make me sweet and speak to them kindly. I have to brag that I got everything I wanted from my husbands.

"My fifth husband, Jenkins, I loved best of all. In fact, I married him for love, and not for his money. He was a clerk who came to live in our town. Now, my fourth husband was still alive when I first met Jenkins, but that did not stop me from planning for the future.

"One day while my husband was in London, Jenkins

and I went walking in the fields. We had a wonderful time and got along very well. I convinced him that I loved him dearly, and I told him that if ever my husband died, he could marry me.

"Not long after that, my fourth husband was carried to his grave. Behind the body walked my Jenkins. He looked so handsome, I immediately fell in love with him. He was twenty and I was forty, but that didn't matter. I still looked young and pretty. During the funeral I managed to cry and look sad like a good wife. But I didn't cry much. I already had my next husband in sight.

"So a month later, Jenkins and I were married. I gave all my land and money into his keeping. That was a mistake. He would not let me have anything I wanted, and he was jealous of me. We quarreled often. I yelled and ranted like a shrew, and I would go out to visit friends just to make him angry.

"Now my husband had a book that he was always reading. Soon he started reading me lectures out of it. He read me stories of wicked, ungrateful wives who killed their husbands or made them go blind or made them set fire to themselves. Some of these wives drove nails into their husbands' brains while they were sleeping. Others put poison in their husbands' food.

"Oh, such horrible stories he told me! And he had sayings, like: 'It is better to live with a lion or a foul dragon than a nagging wife.' All of these were in his big book. And day and night he read to me. Can you imagine the pain this caused me? I was so unhappy!

"Soon I saw that he was never going to stop reading me lectures. One night I got so angry, I suddenly flew at him and ripped three pages out of the book. At the same time, I smacked him so hard that he tipped over backwards into the fire. Up he jumped like an angry lion and hit me on the head so hard that he knocked me out. That is how I came to be deaf in one ear.

"Well, I lay on the floor as though I was dead. When he saw what he had done, he would have fled. But I stopped him. 'Oh,' I said, 'have you murdered me for my lands? But before I die, kiss me!'

"When he saw that I wasn't dead, he knelt beside me and begged my forgiveness. We made up, but not before he had put all the lands, the money, and himself in my power. I made him burn his book first of all. Once I was in control of our house and property, we had no more trouble, and I was a good and true wife to him. But now I will tell you my tale."

Here the Wife of Bath Begins Her Tale

Once upon a time in the days of King Arthur, the world was full of magic. Elves roamed the land, and fairies danced in the meadows.

Now it happened that in his court King Arthur had a knight that all the ladies loved. But this knight committed a wicked deed, and the King said that he must die. He would have surely lost his head, but the Queen and the other ladies begged the King for mercy. So King Arthur gave the knight to the Queen and told her to do as she wished with him. The Queen thanked the King and called the knight to her.

"Sir knight," said the Queen, "it is up to you to save your own neck from the ax. I will grant you your life on one condition. You must tell me the one thing that women desire most. If you cannot answer me now, I will give you a year and a day to seek and learn the answer. But you must promise me that no matter what, you will come back at the end of that time."

So to save his life the knight set out into the world to find what it was that women love most. He went from place to place, from house to house, asking every woman he met. But he never got the same answer twice.

Some women said that they loved riches best. Some said honor. Some said good times. Some said fine clothes. Some said love. Some said marriage. Some wanted to be flattered and pleased. And finally, some said that women want the freedom to do what they please without a nagging husband.

At the end of the year, the poor knight was no closer to the answer than when he started. Sadly, he began his journey home to keep his promise to the Queen. On his way he rode through a forest. Suddenly he saw twenty-four girls dancing in the trees, and he went toward them. He wanted to ask them what they desired most. But right before his eyes, they disappeared. The only person left was an old woman. An uglier hag he had never seen. This old woman stood and greeted him.

"Sir knight," she said, "what can I do for you?"

"Good woman," he replied, "I need your help."

"Tell me what you want, and perhaps I can help you. Old people are wise, you know."

"Old mother," he answered, "I will be a dead man if I can't tell the Queen what it is that women desire most. If you know the answer, I will pay you well."

"I can tell you," she said, "but first you must promise me something."

"Anything!" cried the knight.

"You must promise me that the next thing I ask of you, you will do."

"I promise!" the knight exclaimed.

"Then your life is saved. The Queen and all the other ladies must agree with what I say. Come here, and I will whisper the answer to you."

After she had given him the answer, she told him to be

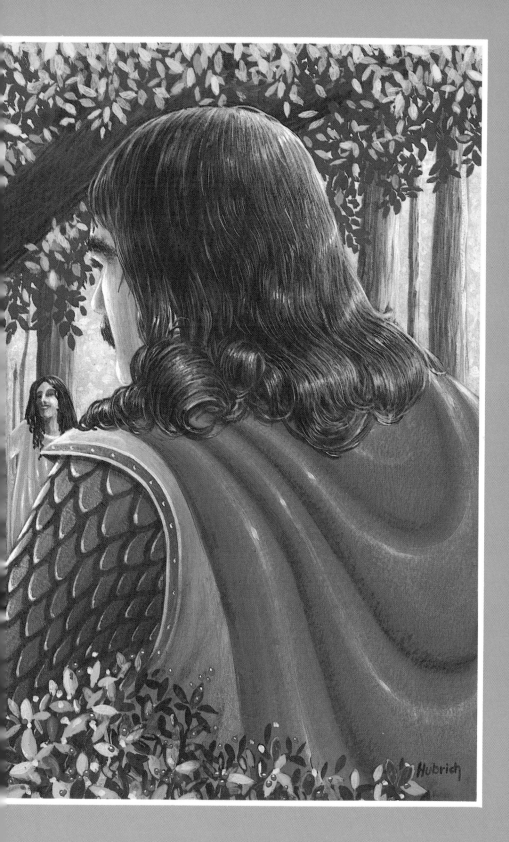

on his way and not to worry. When he arrived back at the Queen's court, all the ladies were there waiting for him.

"Silence!" the Queen ordered the ladies. "Listen to what the knight has to say! Now, Sir knight, speak! What is it that women want most?"

"Here is my answer," said the knight, "and if you do not like it, kill me if you wish."

The room grew very quiet as he said boldly: "What women want most is to be the complete ruler over their husbands and their homes. They want to be the masters of their men!"

Not a woman in the court could deny that his answer was true. They all agreed that the knight was worthy to live.

But just as the knight was given back his life, the old hag appeared. "Now, Sir knight," she cried, "I have saved your life, and you must keep your promise to me."

"What is it you want, old mother?"

"What I ask of you is this," she said. "I want you to marry me!"

"Oh, no!" exclaimed the knight. "Anything but that! Take all my money. Take everything I have, but let me go!"

"No! I am old and ugly and poor, but not for all the money in the world would I give up the chance to be your wife — your love!"

"My love! No, my damnation is more like it!" he cried.

But in the end, he had no choice but to marry the hag. He married her secretly, early one morning so that no one would see his shame. She was so ugly that he couldn't stand to even touch her.

Once alone with his bride, the knight was so miserable that he sat moaning and groaning.

"Dear husband," she said, "what is the matter? What is wrong? Tell me, and I will help you."

"Help me! How? I am a noble, and you are of low birth. I am young, and you are so old and ugly. Is it any wonder I am miserable? I wish I were dead!"

"What is this? What is this?" she asked. "Does my low birth make you miserable? Think, good sir. Since when does being born a noble gentleman or lady make a person good? A noble soul has nothing to do with a person's birth. A lord's son is just as likely to do wicked and shameful deeds as the son of a poor man. A noble character comes from God, and he gives it to all people — not just those born into certain high families.

"You hate me because I am poor," she continued. "Well, let me tell you about poverty. There is no shame in being poor. Our Lord Jesus chose to be poor. Evil comes from the desire for riches. The poor man who is happy learns patience and wisdom. And a poor man knows he has true friends. He knows he is liked for himself and not for his riches. Don't complain to me any more about being poor!

"Now, sir," she went on, "you also say that I am old and ugly. You should be glad! If I were a young and beautiful wife, you would be jealous of me. You would always wonder if I was looking at other men. But since I am so old and ugly, you never need to worry about that. You know that I will be a good and faithful wife to you.

"So now, take your choice," she finished. "Would you rather have me old and ugly as you see me, or would you rather have me lovely and young and always wonder if I am being true to you? Go ahead. The choice is yours."

The knight sighed and thought hard. At last he said: "My lady, my love, my dear wife, I don't know which one to choose. I put myself in your hands. You choose which is best for both of us."

"Since you ask me to make the choice, does that mean I am now your master?" his wife asked.

"Yes, wife," he said. "I think that is the best way."

"If I am your master, then kiss me! For I promise I will be both beautiful and faithful to you. Look and see for yourself!"

And when the knight looked at her, he saw that by magic she had become young and lovely — and his heart was filled with joy. Thus they lived happily ever after.

May the good Lord send all us women meek husbands. May He hurry up the death of husbands who won't be ruled by their wives. And may He send a plague on mean, stingy husbands!

Here ends the wife of Bath's tale. Next to tell his story was the pardoner.

THE PARDONER'S TALE

"Ladies and gentlemen," said the pardoner, "when I speak in churches, my message is always the same: Greed is the cause of all evil. You will see what wickedness greed can bring when I tell you my story."

Here Follows the Pardoner's Tale

Once upon a time three fellows were sitting in a tavern. They were wasting their time with drinking, gambling, and women. As they drank, they heard the funeral bell ring. Outside a body was carried by on its way to the grave. One of the men called his servant.

"Go," he said, "and ask whose body was just carried by."

"I don't have to ask," the servant replied. "It was a friend of yours. Last night he was sitting drunk on his bench. A thief — whom men call Death — slipped in and cut his heart in two and then went away without a word. Watch out for that villain Death, sir. He is a terrible enemy. He has killed thousands of people. You must be prepared to meet him anywhere."

"The boy speaks the truth," said the bartender. "There is a village about a mile from here. Over the past year, Death has killed nearly all of the men, women, and children with the plague. I think he must live there. Be careful of him!"

"What? Is this true?" one of the three men asked. "Is he so dangerous?" He turned to his two companions. "Friends," he said, "let us swear an oath to hunt down this thief Death. Before the night is over, we will find him and kill him."

The three men shook hands and agreed. They would live and die for each other like brothers. Then up they jumped in a drunken rage to go in search of the villain Death. Off they went toward the village where the bartender said he lived. But they had not gone far when they met a poor old man.

"Hey, old man," said one of the three friends, "why have you lived so long?"

"I have traveled from city to city," the old man replied, "and I can't find anyone who will trade his youth for my age. So I must keep my age. Not even Death — alas! — will take my life."

"Old man," said another of the friends, "you speak of Death. That thief has killed so many of our friends. Are you his spy? Tell us where he is!"

"Well, sirs," the old man answered, "if you are so anxious to find Death, turn up that crooked path. I left him in that grove of trees. See that oak tree? You will find him there."

The three friends left the old man and ran to the oak tree. But when they got there, they did not see Death. Instead they found eight bushels of gold coins. They were so happy with all the riches they had found that they forgot all about Death.

"Brothers," said the worst of the three friends, "this is our lucky day! We are rich beyond our wildest dreams.

Now we can spend the rest of our lives spending the gold and living like kings. We will never have to work again. But first we must get the gold home. It wouldn't be safe, though, to carry it during the day. We will have to stay here and wait until dark so no one will see us. Here is my plan then. We will draw straws, and the one who draws the shortest straw will go back into town and buy bread and wine. The other two of us will stay here and guard the gold."

So the three friends drew straws, and the youngest of them drew the short straw. Off he went to town. Once he was gone, one of the men turned to the other and said: "You see all this gold? What would you think if I told you I had a plan? I know a way to keep the gold all for ourselves. We will divide it just between the two of us."

"How can this be?" the other replied.

"It would be easy! There are two of us and only one of our friend. We two are stronger than he. When he returns, you hold him, and I will stab him with my dagger. To be sure he dies, you stab him also. Then the gold will be all ours."

So the two evil friends planned to murder the third.

Meanwhile, the youngest man went on his way into town. He kept thinking of all the beautiful gold. "Oh," he thought, "what if that gold was all mine?" The more he thought about it, the better he liked the idea. And he made his plans.

Once in town he went to the apothecary. "Apothecary," said the young villain, "I am plagued with rats. Also, there is a skunk in my yard that is killing my chickens. I want to buy some poison to kill these creatures and get rid of them this very night."

"I have a poison here," the apothecary answered. "It is so strong that just a tiny drop will kill any creature in the world."

Happily the man bought the poison and ran to the shop next door. There he bought three bottles of wine. In two of these he put the poison. He kept the third bottle to drink himself.

Taking the three bottles, he went back to where his friends waited for him. As soon as the youngest returned with the wine, the two villains jumped on him and killed him, just as they had planned. When this was done, they sat down to rest.

"Let's have something to drink first," one said, "and then we will bury the body and wait for night to come."

He grabbed one of the bottles — one with the poison in it — and took a drink. Then he passed the bottle to his friend. The second man also drank the poisoned wine. In the blink of an eyelid, the two villains lay dead beside their murdered comrade. The old man had spoken the truth. The three men had indeed found Death waiting for them under the oak tree.

So you see, my friends, what greed does to a man. May God forgive you your sins and keep you from being greedy. Perhaps you would like to buy a pardon from me now? Think how lucky you are to have a pardoner with you on your trip. Buy a pardon, and then if you have some accident on the way, you will be safe. Come, have your sins forgiven. Take out your purses and give me your coins.

Here ends the pardoner's tale.

THE CANON YEOMAN'S TALE

After the pardoner had finished his tale, we continued on our way. These jolly tales had made the time pass quickly. We had ridden nearly five miles when we saw two men trying to catch up with us. One was a man dressed all in black. From the hood on his robe, I guessed that he must be a churchman — probably a canon. With him was a yeoman, his servant. Both men had been riding hard. Their horses were covered with sweat and were foaming at the mouth. When the canon reached us, he called out:

"Good people! I have hurried to catch up with you. I would like to ride with such a merry group."

"Sirs," said the yeoman, "I saw you leave the inn this morning. I told my master, because I know he likes to have a good time."

"You are welcome," said our host. "But tell me, yeoman, can your master entertain us with a good story or two?"

"My master?" replied the yeoman. "Of course. He is a jolly man. But he is also sly and sneaky, so beware."

"Here, yeoman," cried the canon. "What are you saying about me? Keep quiet!"

"Go on!" said the host. "Don't let him scare you."

"He doesn't scare me any more. I've had enough of his sneaky ways. I can tell you such stories about him!"

When the canon saw that his servant was about to betray him, he rode quickly away in guilt and shame.

"Now," said the yeoman, "we can have some fun. I'll tell you everything I know. Never again will I work for such a man, no matter how much money he gives me. I have ridden with the canon for seven years, and now I have lost everything I ever had. So have many other good people. Once I was happy and wore fine clothes. Now I am poor. My face is burned from blowing up the coals for the fires.

"The canon, you see, is an alchemist. He claims that he can change cheap metal into gold and silver. Why, people come from miles around just to meet him and try to learn from him the secret of his evil art. But beware of him! He uses tricks and lies to cheat good, honest people. Just listen while I tell you about one man he cheated."

Here Begins the Canon's Yeoman's Tale

In London there lives a priest—a good, pleasant, helpful man. One day the canon went to visit him. He asked the priest to lend him a sum of money.

"Lend me some gold," the canon said, "and I will repay you in three days. If I don't keep my promise, you can have me hanged!"

As I said, the priest was a good man, and he lent the canon the gold. Three days later, the canon returned to pay back the loan. The priest was delighted to find that the canon was such an honest man.

"I don't mind lending you money any time," said the priest. "You are so honest and dependable. You returned the money just when you said you would. You can count on me to lend you money any time."

"What?" said the canon. "Did you think that I would not

keep my promise? No! I have never borrowed money and not returned it just when I said I would. Ask anyone! Why, to take money and not return it on time would be like stealing. I would never be so dishonest to any man. And now, since you have been so good to me, I want to do something for you. If you wish, I will show you some of my secrets of alchemy. I will teach you how I work my art."

"You will?" the priest cried. "You will share your secrets with me?"

"Only if you want me to," the crafty canon replied.

The poor priest was thrilled. He did not realize what he was getting into. The innocent priest was about to be tricked by the greedy canon. Oh, poor stupid priest! Oh, wicked, evil canon!

"Sir," said the canon, "send your servant for some mercury — that cheap metal known as quicksilver. Have him bring two or three ounces. When he returns with it, I will show you a miracle."

"Sir," said the priest, "it shall be done immediately."

The servant left and quickly returned with three ounces of quicksilver and gave them to the canon.

"Now, my good man," said the canon to the servant, "bring me some hot coals so that I can begin my work."

When the servant returned with the coals for the fire, the canon took out a heavy metal bowl from inside his robe.

"Come," he told the priest, "put one ounce of quicksilver into the bowl. Then you shall see my alchemy work. There are not many people I would offer to show my science. But soon you will see this quicksilver changed into real silver, right before your eyes. The silver will be as good and fine as any you have ever had in your purse. First, though, I must add this powder. It is my secret recipe. But before we begin, send your servant away. This secret is just between you and me."

Once the servant was gone, the two men began their

work. They set the bowl on the coals. While the priest blew up the fire, the canon sprinkled the powder in the bowl. I am not sure just what the powder contained. It may have been chalk or ground glass. Whatever it was, it was worthless.

"To show you how I trust you," the canon said, "I will let you do all that must be done."

The priest was delighted. He crouched down and blew harder on the coals as the canon instructed him. While he was busy, the canon — oh, the devil that he was — took out a false coal from inside his robe. He had drilled a hole into the center of it. In that hole he had put one ounce of silver shavings. Then he had sealed the hole with wax so that the silver wouldn't fall out.

"Now," he said to the priest, "we must arrange the coals just so. See? We put them high around the sides of the bowl. But, my friend! You are too hot. You are sweating. Here, take this wet cloth and wipe your face."

While the priest wiped his face, the canon carefully arranged the false coal in just the right place on the edge of the bowl. When it caught fire, the wax would melt and the silver would drop down into the bowl.

Everything went just as he planned. The false coal burned. The wax melted. The silver shavings dropped down into the bowl and began to melt.

"Now," the canon said when all was ready, "we take this mixture and pour it into a pan of cold water to cool it." This he did. "Now! Stick your hand into the pan and see what you find there."

The priest stuck in his hand and pulled out a thin sheet of pure silver.

"God bless you!" exclaimed the priest. "It is silver! I will be your friend forever if you will teach me your wonderful science!"

"We will do it again. Watch closely so you will know how

to do it for yourself. Then when you need silver, you will
know where to get it. Put another ounce of quicksilver into
the bowl."

Once again the canon tricked him. This time he had a
hollow stick filled with just one ounce of silver shavings.
The hole in the end was again stopped up with a piece of
wax. While the priest blew on the coals, the canon threw
in his worthless powder. Then he stirred the mixture with
the hollow stick until the wax melted and the silver pieces
fell out.

When the silver had had time to melt, they again poured
the hot metal into the pan of water. The priest stuck in his
hand a second time and pulled out a thin sheet of silver.

"Oh, this is indeed wonderful!" he cried. "Dear sir,
everything I have is yours for showing me your great
secret."

"Let us try it again," said the sly old canon. "This time
we will use copper instead of quicksilver."

And once again the canon made a fool of the priest. He
added his powder to the copper the priest had put in the
bowl. Once the copper had melted, they poured the mixture into the pan of water. This time the canon reached in
his hand. Here was his trick. He had a thin sheet of silver
hidden up his sleeve. Slyly he pulled it out and dropped it
into the pan. Then he splashed his hand around in the
water and grabbed the copper so quickly that the priest did
not see him.

"Come, my friend," he said to the priest. "Help me.
Stick your hand in with mine and see what you find."

For a third time the priest pulled out a sheet of silver.

"Let us go to the goldsmith," said the crafty canon. "He
will soon be able to tell us if this is fine silver or not."

So they took the three sheets of silver to the goldsmith.
The man tested them and found the sheets to be very fine

silver indeed. No one could have been happier than the stupid priest.

"You must tell me," he pleaded. "How much does your powder cost? I must have it!"

"It is very expensive," said the canon. "No one in all of England knows its secret but me."

"I don't care how much it costs!" the priest cried. "I must have it! Just tell me how much, and I will pay you. Please, I beg you!"

"I will give you the recipe for forty pieces of gold," the canon replied. "And to tell you the truth, if you weren't my friend, it would cost you even more."

Quickly the priest brought the money and gave it to the wicked canon in return for the recipe for the powder.

"I beg you, good priest," the canon said, "to keep this a secret. People would be jealous of my science if they knew. They would surely kill me."

"God forbid!" the priest cried. "I would rather lose everything I have than betray you."

"Ah, you are indeed my friend. And so farewell, good priest. And thank you."

That was the last the foolish priest ever saw of the wicked canon. And when he tried the recipe himself, you can guess what happened. It wouldn't work!

So you see how the canon cheated and tricked the poor, innocent priest. This is the way he brought many men to ruin. So I say to you: Never try to fool with nature. The secret of how to make gold and silver is God's secret. Any man who tries to find that secret is a fool and he will suffer for it. That is my moral.

Here ends the canon's yeoman's tale.

BIOGRAPHICAL NOTE ON GEOFFREY CHAUCER

Records for the Middle Ages are not good, so we are not sure when the English poet Geoffrey Chaucer was born. It was probably around 1342. His parents were middle-class Londoners in the wine business. He was lucky enough, as a child, to become a page to the Countess of Ulster, which meant he was a servant in her household. When he was a teenager he was sent overseas during wars with France, was captured, and then ransomed by the King himself.

Around 1367 Chaucer married. His bride was Philippa de Roet, a lady-in-waiting to the Queen; we think they later had four children. Chaucer was a well-educated man. He could read Latin, French, Anglo-Norman, and Italian, and was an expert in the science of the time. He was also a successful man of the court. He held important business positions in England and traveled to Italy on business for the King. Chaucer also worked for the powerful Duke of Lancaster.

Chaucer was one of the first important writers to write in English; in the Middle Ages the official language in England was usually either Latin or Norman French. Among his other writings is the famous love poem *Troilus and Criseyde*, which is still considered one of the great poems of the English language.

Chaucer died on October 25, 1400, leaving *The Canterbury Tales* unfinished. He is buried in Westminister Abbey in London. Today he is often called the Father of English Poetry.

GLOSSARY

alchemy (al' kə mē)   a science of the Middle Ages that claimed the power to turn common metals into gold or silver

apothecary (ə päth' ə ker ē)   someone who sells drugs and medicines

canon (kan' ən)   a churchman who works for a cathedral

pardoner (pärd' ə nər)   a preacher of the Middle Ages who sold religious objects, and often claimed the power to pardon people for their sins in exchange for money

pilgrimage (pil' grə mij)   a journey to a shrine or sacred place

quicksilver (kwik' sil vər)   another name for the element mercury; a silver-colored heavy liquid

tavern (tav' ərn)   a place where liquor and food are sold

yeoman (yō' mən)   a servant to another person

45